Think BiG!

NANCY CARLSON

Carolrhoda Books, Inc./Minneapolis

Carolrhoda Books, Inc.
A division of Lerner Publishing Group
241 First Avenue North
Minneapolis, MN 55401 U.S.A.

Website address: www.lernerbooks.com

Library of Congress Cataloging-in-Publication Data

Carlson, Nancy.
    Think big! / by Nancy Carlson.
        p.   cm.
    Summary: Vinney is frustrated about being one of the smallest
children at school, but when he takes his mother's advice and
thinks big for a day, he discovers that there are advantages to
being small.
    ISBN-13: 978-1-57505-622-7 (lib. bdg. : alk. paper)
    ISBN-10: 1-57505-622-4 (lib. bdg. : alk. paper)
    [1. Size—Fiction. 2. Schools—Fiction. 3. Self-esteem—Fiction.]
I. Title.
PZ7.C21665Th 2005
[E]—dc22   2003027200

Manufactured in the United States of America
2 3 4 5 6 7 - JR - 11 10 09 08 07 06

To my friends at
The Red Balloon Bookstore
in St. Paul, Minnesota!
Thanks for selling my books
for 20 years!

When Vinney came home from school, Mom asked, "How was your day?"
"Not so good," said Vinney.

"On the way to school, George called me shrimp!"

"At the library, I couldn't reach the chapter books.

The big kids took my four square ball at recess."

"And the lunch lady didn't even see me standing in line!

I'm so small, my teacher didn't see me raising my hand. When she finally noticed me, I got the smallest part in the class play—"

"And I'm a great shot!

Being small is no fun."

"Vinney," said Mom, "someday you'll be bigger. But until then, you'll just have to THINK BIG."

The next morning, Vinney jumped out of bed.
"Today I'm going to THINK BIG!"

On the way to school,
George still said,
"Hiya shrimp!"

Vinney kept thinking big and said, "How's the weather up there?"

When Vinney went to the library, he told himself to think big and chose a huge chapter book.

But Vinney discovered he wasn't ready for big chapter books. So the librarian found a book that was the perfect size for him.

He lost, but it was lots of fun!

At lunch, Vinney was determined to make the lunch lady notice him. He walked through the line on his tippy-toes. "You look like you have a big appetite," the lunch lady said.

Then she gave him an extra piece of pizza and two cookies to help him grow!

Vinney thought as big as he could when his teacher needed a helper, and she picked him to clean the blackboard—

even though he could only reach half of it!

During play practice, Vinney even sang big. So his
teacher gave him a bigger part—Prince Charming!

But when Vinney had to kiss the princess,
he wished he was a ladybug again.
"Yuck!" thought Vinney.

Vinney remembered to think big in gym class,
and he grabbed the basketball.

"No one can catch me!" thought Vinney.

He dribbled the ball right into Cody, the biggest kid in his class! "Uh oh! It's time to think . . ."

"SMALL!"
Vinney ran right under Cody's legs and scored a three pointer!

When Vinney got home, Mom asked, "Did you think big today?"
"I sure did," said Vinney. "Thinking big is great, but . . ."

"sometimes I'm glad to be small."